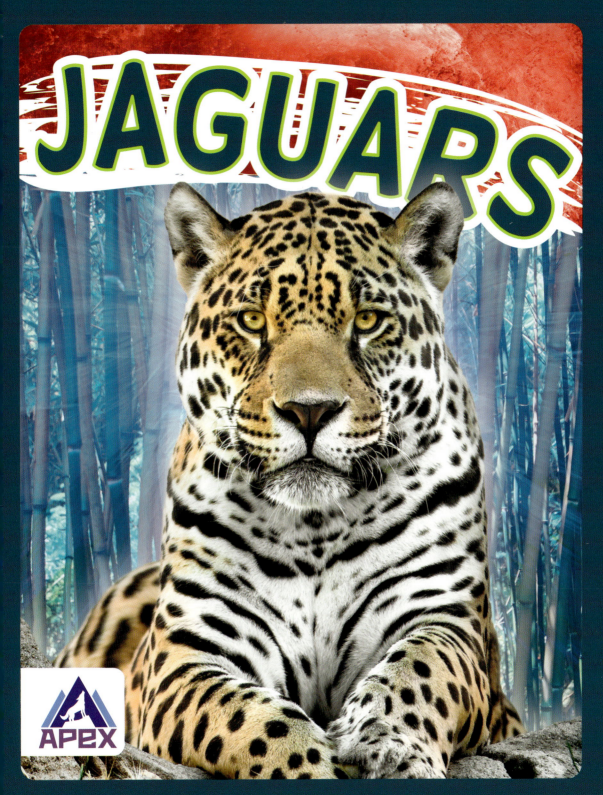

JAGUARS

By Sophie Geister-Jones

WWW.APEXEDITIONS.COM

Copyright © 2022 by Apex Editions, Mendota Heights, MN 55120. All rights reserved. No part of this book may be reproduced or utilized in any form or by any means without written permission from the publisher.

Apex is distributed by North Star Editions:
sales@northstareditions.com | 888-417-0195

Produced for Apex by Red Line Editorial.

Photographs ©: Shutterstock Images, cover, 1, 4–5, 6–7, 8, 9, 10–11, 12–13, 14, 15, 16–17, 18–19, 20, 21, 22–23, 24–25, 26, 27, 29

Library of Congress Control Number: 2020952946

ISBN
978-1-63738-030-7 (hardcover)
978-1-63738-066-6 (paperback)
978-1-63738-134-2 (ebook pdf)
978-1-63738-102-1 (hosted ebook)

Printed in the United States of America
Mankato, MN
082021

NOTE TO PARENTS AND EDUCATORS

Apex books are designed to build literacy skills in striving readers. Exciting, high-interest content attracts and holds readers' attention. The text is carefully leveled to allow students to achieve success quickly. Additional features, such as bolded glossary words for difficult terms, help build comprehension.

TABLE OF CONTENTS

CHAPTER 1
ATTACK IN THE WATER 5

CHAPTER 2
LIFE IN THE WILD 11

CHAPTER 3
STRONG BODIES 17

CHAPTER 4
HOW JAGUARS HUNT 23

Comprehension Questions • 28

Glossary • 30

To Learn More • 31

About the Author • 31

Index • 32

CHAPTER 1
ATTACK IN THE WATER

A jaguar glides through the water. A large **caiman** is sunning itself on the shore. The jaguar has her eyes on the **reptile**. She is hungry.

Jaguars can hunt animals that weigh four times more than they do.

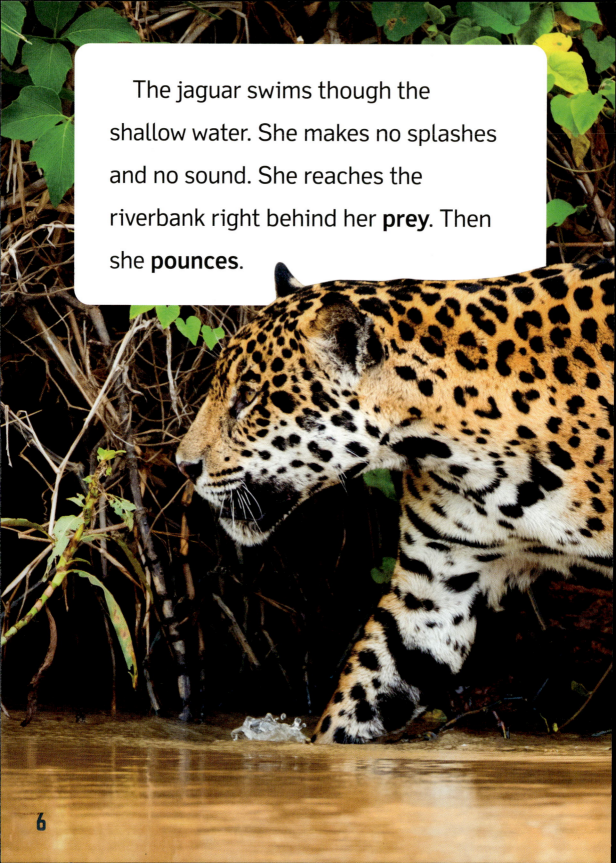

The jaguar swims though the shallow water. She makes no splashes and no sound. She reaches the riverbank right behind her **prey**. Then she **pounces**.

The jaguar lands on the caiman's back. She bites and claws it. The reptile thrashes. But the jaguar kills it. Then she begins to eat.

Jaguars eat many kinds of animals, including reptiles, fish, birds, and deer.

A jaguar has a line of spots down its back.

STRONG SWIMMERS

Unlike some cats, jaguars love water. They swim in lakes and rivers. In fact, they often hunt in or near the water.

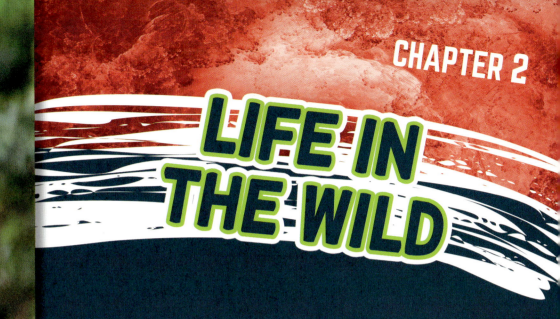

CHAPTER 2
LIFE IN THE WILD

Jaguars can live in many different places. Some jaguars live in **swamps** or forests. Others live in grasslands.

Jaguars often live in places with many trees.

11

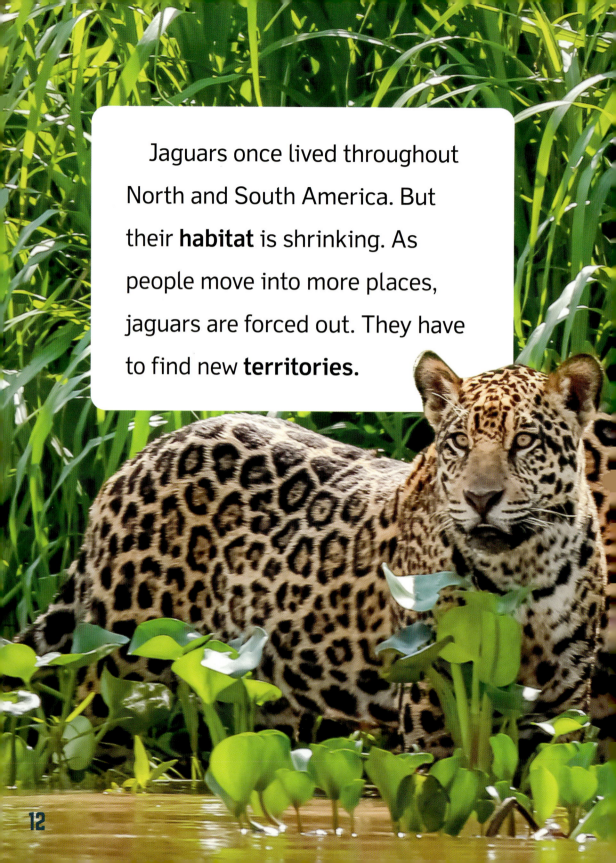

Jaguars once lived throughout North and South America. But their **habitat** is shrinking. As people move into more places, jaguars are forced out. They have to find new **territories.**

Today, most jaguars live in the Amazon **rain forest**. But people are cutting down trees. They sell the wood or clear land for cattle farms. Jaguars and other animals lose their homes.

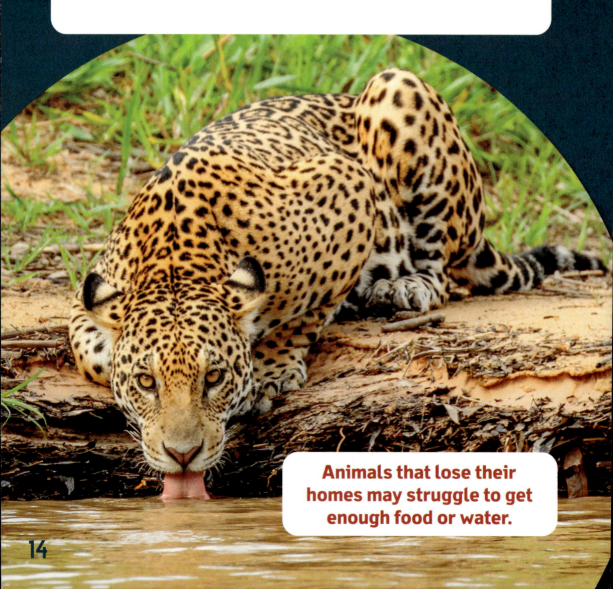

Animals that lose their homes may struggle to get enough food or water.

Jaguars have two to four cubs at a time.

RAISING BABIES

Animals need space to raise babies. Jaguar cubs are born in dens. Their mother protects the cubs. She hides them from danger. Later, she teaches them how to hunt.

STRONG BODIES

Jaguars have large heads and short legs. They have strong muscles. Their sharp claws help them climb trees. And their large paws help them swim.

A male jaguar can weigh up to 265 pounds (120 kg).

Jaguars have sharp teeth and strong jaws. They can bite through thick skin and shells.

Jaguars have stronger bites than all other big cats.

A jaguar's large, pointed teeth help tear food.

A jaguar's fur is usually orange, white, or tan. Its body is covered in dark spots.

A jaguar's spots are called rosettes.

Each jaguar's spots are unique. No two cats have the same pattern.

Some jaguars look all black. But these cats still have spots.

JAGUAR OR LEOPARD?

Jaguars and leopards look very similar. Both cats have black spots. But the shape of the spots is slightly different. Jaguars have a black dot inside each spot. Leopards do not.

CHAPTER 4
HOW JAGUARS HUNT

Jaguars live alone. Each cat has its own territory. The cat hunts and **roams** in this area.

The word *jaguar* means "he who kills with one leap."

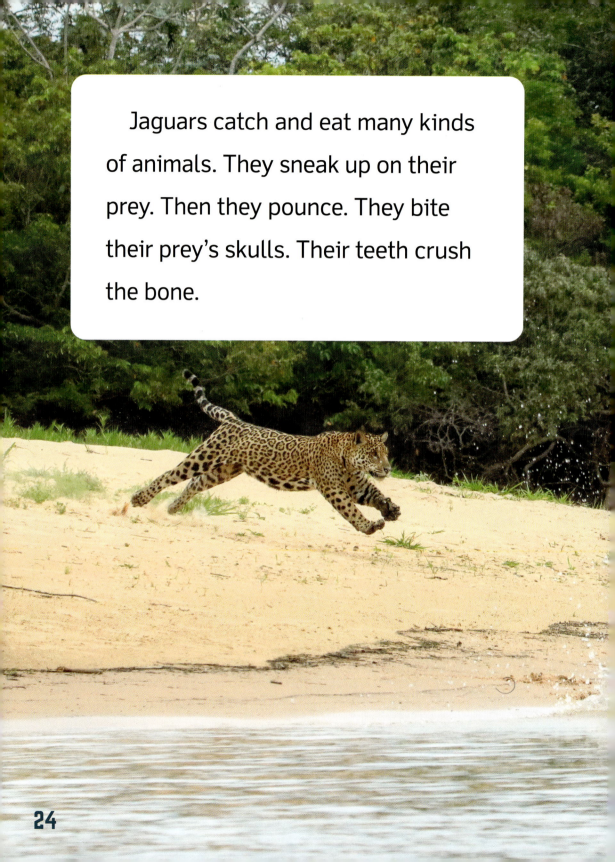

Jaguars catch and eat many kinds of animals. They sneak up on their prey. Then they pounce. They bite their prey's skulls. Their teeth crush the bone.

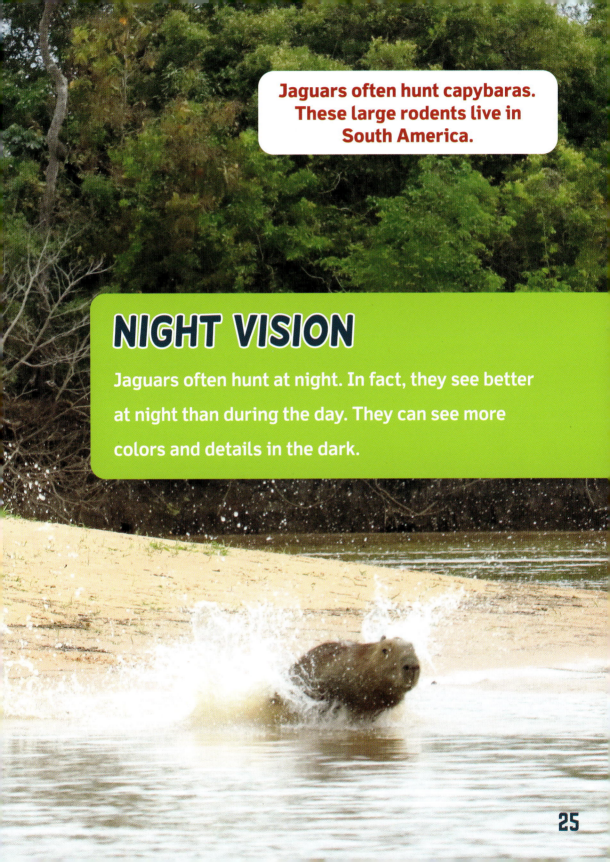

Jaguars often hunt capybaras. These large rodents live in South America.

NIGHT VISION

Jaguars often hunt at night. In fact, they see better at night than during the day. They can see more colors and details in the dark.

Jaguars often hunt caiman and turtles. Sometimes, jaguars catch fish. They dangle their tails in the water to **attract** fish. When fish come close, jaguars grab them.

Jaguars sometimes climb trees and jump down on prey below.

Jaguars often rest on the branches of trees.

COMPREHENSION QUESTIONS

Write your answers on a separate piece of paper.

1. Write a few sentences describing how jaguars hunt their prey.

2. Jaguars are good swimmers. Do you enjoy spending time in the water? Why or why not?

3. How are jaguar and leopard spots different?
   - **A.** Leopard spots have a dot in the middle.
   - **B.** Jaguar spots have a dot in the middle.
   - **C.** Jaguar spots are not dark.

4. Why would cutting down trees in the Amazon harm jaguars?
   - **A.** Jaguars live and hunt among the trees.
   - **B.** Jaguars use the trees to build nests.
   - **C.** Jaguars eat the trees.

5. What does **unique** mean in this book?

*Each jaguar's spots are **unique**. No two cats have the same pattern.*

   A. exactly the same
   B. different from all others
   C. not possible to see

6. What does **protects** mean in this book?

*Their mother **protects** the cubs. She hides them from danger.*

   A. hurts something
   B. keeps something safe
   C. sends something away

Answer key on page 32.

GLOSSARY

attract
To make something come closer.

caiman
An alligator-like animal that lives in water.

habitat
The type of place where animals normally live.

pounces
Jumps on something to catch it.

prey
An animal that is hunted and eaten by another animal.

rain forest
An area with many trees and lots of rain.

reptile
A cold-blooded animal that has scales.

roams
Moves throughout a large area.

swamps
Areas of low land covered in water, often with many plants.

territories
Areas that animals or groups of animals live in and defend.

TO LEARN MORE

BOOKS

Adamson, Thomas K. *Anaconda vs. Jaguar.* Minneapolis: Bellwether Media, 2020.

Grack, Rachel. *Jaguars.* Minneapolis: Bellwether Media, 2019.

Olson, Elsie. *Animal Predator Smackdown.* Minneapolis, Abdo Publishing, 2020.

ONLINE RESOURCES

Visit **www.apexeditions.com** to find links and resources related to this title.

ABOUT THE AUTHOR

Sophie Geister-Jones lives in Saint Paul, Minnesota. She loves reading. She and her brothers have a book club.

INDEX

B
biting, 8, 18, 24

C
claws, 17
cubs, 15

F
fish, 27
forests, 11
fur, 20

G
grasslands, 11

H
habitat, 12
hunting, 9, 15, 23, 25, 27

J
jaws, 18

P
paws, 17
pouncing, 6, 24
prey, 6, 24, 27

R
rain forest, 14

S
spots, 20–21
swamps, 11

T
teeth, 18, 24
territories, 12–13, 23
trees, 13–14, 17, 27

W
water, 5–6, 9, 27

Answer Key:
1. Answers will vary; **2.** Answers will vary; **3.** B; **4.** A; **5.** B; **6.** B